I Be Emma

I Be Emma

Charlotte Pritchard

iUniverse, Inc.
Bloomington

I Be Emma

Copyright © 2013 by Charlotte Pritchard.

All rights reserved. No part of this book may be used or reproduced by any means, graphic, electronic, or mechanical, including photocopying, recording, taping or by any information storage retrieval system without the written permission of the publisher except in the case of brief quotations embodied in critical articles and reviews.

This is a work of fiction. All of the characters, names, incidents, organizations, and dialogue in this novel are either the products of the author's imagination or are used fictitiously.

iUniverse books may be ordered through booksellers or by contacting:

iUniverse
1663 Liberty Drive
Bloomington, IN 47403
www.iuniverse.com
1-800-Authors (1-800-288-4677)

Because of the dynamic nature of the Internet, any web addresses or links contained in this book may have changed since publication and may no longer be valid. The views expressed in this work are solely those of the author and do not necessarily reflect the views of the publisher, and the publisher hereby disclaims any responsibility for them.

Any people depicted in stock imagery provided by Thinkstock are models, and such images are being used for illustrative purposes only.
Certain stock imagery © Thinkstock.

ISBN: 978-1-4759-7805-6 (sc)
ISBN: 978-1-4759-7806-3 (ebk)

Library of Congress Control Number: 2013904056

Printed in the United States of America

iUniverse rev. date: 03/19/2013

"Emma, would you please put this sweater on my bed before you go and play?" asked Bess as she ripped open the first of two envelopes. As she sat down to read the letter, Emma ran past her for the door. "Stay on the porch and play, okay?"

"Okay," replied three-year-old Emma as the screen door slammed behind her. Dodger, the yellow lab, was at Emma's heels.

Bess's attention was on the two letters that were delivered this morning by Mr. Jetter on his weekly mail route. She didn't notice that the door hadn't closed properly when Emma slammed it shut.

One of the letters was from her sister Agnes back in Ohio. The other letter was from her brother who was fighting overseas. The first letter she received from him was a month ago. After three weeks of fighting, he was in a hospital in Italy recovering from being shot twice in his left arm. Muscle and bone were almost gone. Now the arm was rendered useless.

Thanks a lot, President Wilson, she thought to herself. Her brother Elwin enlisted a week after President Wilson declared in April 1917 that the United States would be entering the war.

The letter she was holding was seven weeks old and addressed from Germany. *He must be out of the hospital now and hopefully coming home*, she thought as she opened the envelope.

Bess and Jake Taggert had moved to Tennessee from Ohio six years ago. They wanted a quiet place to raise a family, and since both were nature enthusiasts, moving to this semiremote location seemed ideal. They lived along Logger's Road, which was once the main road for loggers traveling to the mill in Jaspar. They were close enough to the city of Jaspar to take advantage of the services offered there. The mill closed a year before Jake and Bess moved, and now there were five families living along the road. The closest neighbor lived a mile away, and the farthest neighbor lived fifteen miles away.

Their new home had been abandoned for three years before they moved in. The walls of the house were still sturdy, but repairs needed to be done to the porch and roof. There were five rooms that needed a fresh look. Bess decided the two bedrooms would need new wallpaper, and the remaining rooms would get a good paint job. Thankfully, the repairs were completed before Emma was born three years later. Bess was pregnant with their second child and hoped this baby would be a boy.

As Bess was reading the letter, she felt a nudge on her hand and noticed that Dodger was standing beside her chair. She absently petted him, still reading the letter. Dodger once again nudged her hand.

"What's the matter, old boy? Is Emma ignoring you again?"

I Be Emma

Assuming that Emma had come into the house since Dodger was beside her, she called out for her.

"Emma! Dodger wants your company!" Dodger and Emma were inseparable.

Bess got up and walked toward Emma's room.

"Emma?" she called.

"Where are you?"

The room was empty. Dodger was right behind Bess as she turned toward the door. "Emma!" she called again.

She opened the screen door and saw that Emma wasn't playing on the porch. Her doll was lying on one of the steps.

Where did that girl go? she wondered. She stepped off the porch and went to the side of the house, thinking Emma was by the chicken coop. She wasn't there, so once again Bess called out for her.

Bess scanned the yard but didn't see her. She turned toward the porch again but saw no sign of her daughter. A cold fear filled her and caught in her throat, making her feel like she was choking. She ran to the porch and started pulling the rope to the dinner bell. She screamed Emma's name over and over.

Tears were streaming down her cheeks. She knew that Jake would hear the bell and realize that it wasn't dinner she was ringing about. It was too early for that. He would stop windrowing and come running to the house. Her panic was overbearing, and she screamed harder with each tug of the rope, calling Emma's name.

"Emma!"

Seven Years Later

Clara looked down at the dirt road. The footpath she had just traveled on ended here at the side of the road. She looked to her left and saw that the road went into a curve that disappeared into a grove of trees. She looked to the right. The road went up a hill and disappeared. She looked back down at the road in front of her. Dare she step onto the road? What if it disappeared from under her? If the road disappeared, then she would know that what she had seen yesterday was just her imagination. She slowly moved her foot to take a step. She quickly pulled back and let out a small sigh. *Better be safe*, she thought.

She had seen the neighbor, Frank Stoddard, and his son, Bennie, take this path many times. The path started at the Stoddard house and went past Clara's house. She traveled the path to the Stoddard home many times but never went beyond her home in the opposite direction. Yesterday morning, she had seen Frank and Bennie walking down the path, and curiosity finally took hold of her.

Where do they go? she wondered.

Yesterday, she had been able to get away from the house. Her mother, Mattie Collins, usually kept a close eye on Clara, but Mattie had fallen asleep. Clara was going to see where the path led to.

She had never ventured this far from home, but determination made her keep going until she had made it to the road where the path ended. Mattie had always warned her never to go any farther than to the Stoddards'. She was afraid of Clara having contact with other people; it could result in Clara being taken away from her and Ed. No one was to know that Clara wasn't their biological child.

Clara had decided to return home but then spotted a blackberry bush. She took a couple of berries and popped them into her mouth, enjoying the sweet taste. She decided to gather some to take home, hoping this would prevent the scolding that she knew would be waiting for her. By now, her mother was surely awake and looking for her. Clara started

I Be Emma

to gather the berries when she spotted someone coming over the hill.

Thankfully, the bush concealed most of her as she quickly stepped back and squatted down. She hid partially behind the bush and watched as the girl came walking down the hill on the dirt road. The girl obviously didn't see Clara; she walked right past her and took the turn that disappeared into the grove of trees.

Clara sat there as if in a trance. She knew there were other people—but not in this remote area of Tennessee. She had always imagined them living far away from there. On one or two occasions, a hunter would come to their home. They were usually lost and thirsty. Pa would accommodate them and enjoyed talking with them. He would ask a lot of questions and always seemed satisfied with the answers given to him. After their visits, he always had interesting stories to tell.

Who would she be and where did she come from? thought Clara. She tried to remember if anyone had ever mentioned there being other people there. All she knew were Frank, Ida, Bennie, and Ma and Pa. Surely if there were other people there they would have met by now and visited with each other. Clara was baffled. She would ask Ma and Pa.

Clara slowly got up and looked down the dirt road. Did Frank and Bennie visit this girl? Surely she would have parents. She looked to be about the same age as Clara.

Now, the following afternoon, Clara stood at the edge of the road and looked to the hill. She went to the blackberry bush that had hidden her the day before and tucked herself behind it. She had a good view of the road, so if the girl came again, she would see her. She picked some berries and put them in the pail she had brought with her today. It was easy for her to get out of the house again today. Her mother had been very pleased with the blackberries and agreed to let Clara pick more. Clara smiled. She was eager to meet this girl. The thought of someone her own age appealed to her.

She had no idea if the girl would walk by again or if she had just imagined her. She held her breath for a second or two and whispered, "Please, please, please."

Another minute or so went by, and to Clara's delight, she saw the girl heading in her direction. Clara sat watching her, and when the girl was close enough, Clara stood up and yelled, "Hey, girl!"

The girl froze and stood staring at Clara. Clara took a step forward.

"Where did you come from?" asked the girl. "Who are you?"

"From yonder," Clara said, pointing behind her while still looking at the girl. Clara walked toward her and got about as close as she dared. "I be Clara Collins. I live back in the woods over there." Then she pointed toward the hill, from where the girl had come. "What's yonder?"

"I'm Marissa Campbell. I haven't seen you before. I go to the school just over the hill. You aren't in school. You sure you live around here? Why aren't you in school? How old are you?" Marissa was becoming curious. She couldn't imagine anyone not being in school. She took a good look at Clara and was somewhat dismayed at what she saw. Clara looked very thin, and her clothes, face, and hands were dirty. She wore no shoes, and her hair was in a long, messy braid.

She's one of those backwoods people, Marissa thought to herself. *No wonder she isn't in school.* She had heard people talk about them as being ignorant, lazy, and good-for-nothings, and here she was talking with one of them.

As Marissa was taking a good look at Clara, Clara was also taking a good look at Marissa, who had short hair and was wearing a pretty green dress. She saw the girl's black shoes and

I Be Emma

wondered what it would be like to have real shoes. All she had was a pair of homemade shoes. They were soft leather with double layers of the leather for the sole of the shoe, and she wore them when the weather was cold.

Clara's interest piqued when she heard the word "school." "You get schooling?"

Clara noticed the books that Marissa was carrying. She wanted to read more than anything. Her pa once read a story to her. It was so long ago she didn't remember what the story was about. Pa had never read to her since. Ma wouldn't allow it. Ma said she didn't need schooling and that she needed to learn how to take care of a home and take care of Ma and Pa when Clara got hitched to Bennie when she turned fifteen. She had no idea what being hitched meant and could only imagine being tied with a rope to Bennie and following him around just like their mule, Jezebel, when hitched to a wagon.

"How old are you?" Marissa asked again.

"I be ten."

"That's the same age as me."

"Really?" Clara said with delight. "I never knowed anyone the same age as me. Where do you live? You always come from over the hill like that? What's this schooling like? You know how to read?" Questions seemed to pile up in Clara's mind, and she couldn't get them all out as fast as she wanted.

Marissa started laughing. "Stop, stop. One question at a time."

Clara smiled as she listened to Marissa's soft laugh. Suddenly she wanted to have her as a friend. "Will you be my friend?" she asked quickly.

Marissa looked puzzled. "Don't you have friends? What about your brothers and sisters? Do you have brothers and sisters?"

"No. It's just me and Ma and Pa. We have neighbors, and they have a boy named Bennie. I don't know any girls. You be the first girl I see." Suddenly, Clara seemed to sense that a lot of time had passed. "I best be going home."

"Wait—will I see you tomorrow?"

Clara knew that was going to be impossible. Being gone from the house two days in a row was about as lucky as she could get. "I reckon I be back here sometime. Don't know when. I do be wanting to see you again."

Clara walked back to the blackberry bushes and picked up her pail. She turned and waved at Marissa and headed into the woods.

Clara tried to think of a way to see Marissa again. She knew the blackberry story wasn't going to work. There were fewer berries than yesterday. Too many birds were around picking at them.

I don't know how I'll do it, but maybe something will come to mind, she thought as she ran the rest of the way home.

Clara's home sat deep into the woods from the dirt road. There was a small clearing east of the house where Clara's pa, Ed Collins, had a small field for hay and corn. The garden patch sat at the south end of the field.

Between the house and the field was a wagon-tracked road that went to the north. Pa always traveled that road to the main road when he went to peddle the brooms that he made. A shed sat to the left of the road. The house was unpainted and had a worn look to it, as if a strong wind could topple it over in a few seconds. A lean-to for the chickens was supported by the north side of the house, and a smokehouse stood just behind the coop. Going along the house on both sides were thick bushes that stopped at the front of the house. A porch extended the length of the front of the house.

The path that Clara took earlier that day came from the south past the porch and kept going to the west of the house.

I Be Emma

Her mother, Mattie Collins, was outside sitting and peeling potatoes when she got to the house.

"Been away from the house too long, missy," Mattie warned. "There be things that need to get done before your pa comes in for supper." Clara knew now it was going to be impossible to leave the house anytime soon. "Let me see what you done get," Mattie continued. She reached for the pail, and Clara handed it over.

"It took you this long to get just this much? The way you was talking yesterday, that pail should be filled to the top." She shoved the pail back at Clara.

"I fell asleep."

"Well, you falling asleep or not, it was too long from here. I need you to help around here. Can't do it all myself. You need to learn to keep house, not falling asleep when you want. Go take them and put them in a bowl. Get to cleaning that corn. Pa brought them in from the field. When you get done with that, I need to have water brought in from the well."

Clara went into the house, letting Ma ramble on about the work around there. She had heard the same story over and over. Ma always had something to complain about. Pa would just shake his head, pat Ma on the back, and say, "Now, Ma. Things will turn out the way they supposed to be." This would make Ma all the more agitated, but Pa never stopped saying it.

Clara absently husked the corn. She thought about her day and meeting Marissa. She was excited to have a friend her age. She would have liked to tell Ma and Pa about her but knew she had better keep it a secret for now.

I have a new friend, she thought and gave a little giggle. Just then, Pa came into the room.

Ed Collins was a soft-spoken man with a laid-back attitude that irritated Mattie frequently. He had mentioned that Clara should have schooling, but Mattie refused to listen. She wanted Clara to learn to take care of a home so she and Pa would be taken care of in their old age and wouldn't be alone. Schooling wasn't going to teach Clara how to take care of a home. She had become more aware of that when Ida told her about their daughter, Sarah, going to a fancy school in the city; since then, she hadn't come home.

"What good is that?" Ma fumed. "Besides, I already talked this out with Frank and Ida, as you know. So when Clara turns fifteen, she and Bennie will get hitched."

Clara had heard that argument between the two of them now and again. All she wanted was to learn to read. She couldn't think of what harm that would cause. She had asked Pa if he would teach her to read, and he just shook his head. He didn't want to agitate Mattie more than she already was about the subject.

"What you giggling about?" Pa asked with a smile as he laid his hat on the table.

"Oh, it just be the silk from this here corn that be tickling me."

He walked by and patted her on the head as he headed back to the door. She could hear Ma already complaining to Pa about her being away from the house too long. She tuned them out and continued to husk.

Marissa gets schooling, and she should teach me to read, Clara decided as she put the last ear of corn in the kettle. The prospect of that excited Clara.

The next morning, however, Clara realized that she might not be able to see Marissa again anytime soon. She was suddenly afraid that Marissa would forget her or stop walking down the hill to where they had met. Her mind created all sorts of scenarios.

As her fear and longing grew, she decided to take a chance and go to see Marissa that afternoon. She spent the morning

I Be Emma

doing laundry as the day got hotter and hotter. She had just hung the last of the clothes on the line and noticed that Ma was sitting in her chair on the porch. She walked toward her to tell her that she was done but noticed that Ma had fallen asleep. Clara didn't know how long she had been asleep, but if she was going to see Marissa, this was the time.

She started walking backward away from the house, looking at Ma to make sure she didn't wake up. She got past the big bush that hid the house from the dirt path and then started running. She ran as fast as she could toward the dirt road where she had met Marissa.

When she finally made it, she looked toward the hill where Marissa had come from. She had no idea if she had already walked by, but she stood there looking and waiting. *Can't wait much longer. Ma be waking up.*

After a few minutes, she gave up. Feeling disappointed, she turned to go back home. She took another look toward the hill and saw nothing. As she turned to go back, she saw a piece of paper sticking to the blackberry bush. She took the paper off the branch and noticed writing on it. Since she had no idea what it said, she was puzzled. She turned the paper over and back again. She had a feeling that it was from Marissa. That lifted her spirits for a moment—but then they plummeted.

"I don't be knowing how to read," she said. "I don't read," she said again with a disgusted anger.

She folded the paper, put it in her pocket, and ran back to the house.

To Clara's relief, Ma was still asleep. Clara went to her room, took the paper from her pocket, and smoothed it out on the bed. She looked at every letter, hoping that somehow she could read it. It was useless, but at least she knew now that Marissa hadn't forgotten her. She would probably look to see if the paper was still on the bush. She would see it was gone.

She would then know that Clara hadn't forgotten her. Clara felt a little better and looked for a place to hide the paper. There was a hole in the wall next to her bed, so she stuck the paper in there.

A thought came to her. *If I can get Pa to help me . . .*

She took the paper out of the hole. She decided she would copy some of the writing and somehow show it to Pa and have him tell her what it said.

She went into the kitchen and found a pencil lying next to the matchbox by the stove. She needed to find some paper, but where? She looked around the kitchen but saw none. She went into the other room and went over to Pa's chair. *If there be any paper here, it would be by Pa's chair.* She looked down by the chair leg and saw a piece. She grabbed it and ran to her bedroom.

As best she could, she started copying what she saw. She had no idea if she was making a word. After copying a few letters, she stopped, hoping what she had copied was a word. She folded the paper and put it back in the hole. She was getting excited. She was finally going to know what a word meant. She wished to know all of them, but she had to be careful. She had to figure out how to get Pa to help her without Ma finding out.

Several weeks had gone by since Clara met Marissa. Pa would be peddling his brooms soon, and Clara still hadn't found out what the words were she had copied. Her chance came one afternoon.

"Clara," Pa said as he got up from the kitchen table, "there be a ball of twine in the shed. Get that for me and help me bundle up some straw."

"Yes, Pa." *Finally*, thought Clara. *Now be my chance.*

I Be Emma

She quickly went into her bedroom and took the paper that she had copied letters on and put it in her pocket.

She went to the shed, got the twine, and followed Pa to the back of the shed. She sat down beside him and started bundling small amounts of straw together. Frank Stoddard whittled the broom handles and never asked for a payment from Ed. It was just understood between the two that when he supplied Ed with the broom handles, Ed would supply Frank and his family with the homemade shoes that Mattie bound together.

Ed would be making trips around the county to stores in the towns and also to homes up in the hills where it was hard for families to make trips into the towns. Clara had never been allowed to go with him when he made these trips. Ma felt she was too young to be away from the house for a week or two. Clara was hoping she was old enough to go with him the next time he was ready to sell some brooms. She knew that it would be a good time to ask him about reading. Maybe without Ma being around, he would be willing to help her. But today she wanted to know what she had on her paper.

They didn't talk much. Each of them was busy measuring out the straw that would make up a broom. At a young age, Clara had been taught how to get a bundle together and how much straw was needed. She had learned quickly from him what was needed to make a broom.

After doing a few bundles, she paused for a few seconds.

I just need to ask, she thought. She took the paper out of her pocket, unfolded it, and held it up to Pa. "What this be saying?"

"What you got here?" he asked as he took the paper from her. "Doesn't say much, just a word or two. Where did you get it?"

"I found it."

"Well, the two words say, 'looking for.' Odd kind of message," he said absently.

"Point to the two words, please?"

"Well, this one here is 'looking,' and this one is 'for.' Whoever wrote that be looking for something, I reckon."

Clara looked at the two words. She was going to memorize them so that if she saw them again she would know what they were. She felt happy, thinking that Marissa was looking for her. *That had to be it. She was looking for me*, she thought to herself.

Clara and Pa continued getting the bundles ready for the brooms. They worked all afternoon, and the bundles piled up between them.

"I think I have enough here to make quite a few brooms. Bring in good money for the winter supplies. I be starting tomorrow to make 'em. Hope to start traveling by the end of next week with 'em."

"Pa, can I go with? I be old enough to help."

"Well . . . seems you might be, at that." Pa laughed.

That was music to Clara's ears. She sat looking at him with the biggest smile she had ever made.

Clara was able to make one more trip down to the dirt road. To her delight, she got to see Marissa.

"I be so excited to see you. I be wanting to learn to read. You get schooling, and you can teach me how to read. I be wanting to know."

"No wonder I didn't get a note from you. I had looked and looked for one, and now I know why. Do you know the alphabet? You know, like the ABCs?"

Clara just looked at her. "I know nothing."

Marissa took a piece of paper and started writing down the alphabet. When she finished, she recited them to Clara.

I Be Emma

"These letters make words. Once you know them, you can write anything you want."

They went over the letters again and again. Finally Marissa wrote Clara's name and told Clara to say the word.

Slowly, Clara repeated the letters.

"Now what does that sound like? Do it again."

Again Clara repeated the letters. She concentrated on each sound and finally figured out that what she saw was her name. Clara shrieked with excitement.

"You did it. It's your name. Let me write some more words. You can practice sounding them out. In no time, you'll be reading a book." Marissa gave a little laugh. "You sure are excited to learn. Next time I see you, we can learn more. I better go now. My mother will be wondering why it's taking so long for me to get home."

"Where do you live?" asked Clara.

"Just around the corner." She pointed to the curve of the road. "Sometime, if you can, I'll take you to my house."

Clara smiled and took the paper from Marissa and put it in her pocket. She watched as Marissa started walking down the road. "Bye!" Clara called out.

"Bye!" Marissa called back and waved.

Clara returned home and was hoping to go to her room to look over the paper. Ma was waiting for her instead.

"You be wasting the day away. Get to scrubbing those pans, missy. I be wondering what gets into you sometimes." Ma shook her head and walked out the door.

As Clara scrubbed away, she quietly repeated the letters she had learned. She said them over and over. By the time she had finished, she could almost repeat them backward.

Pa came into the kitchen.

"I be looking for you. We be leaving in two days. I had a hard time convincing your ma to let you go, but I assured her you would be safe with me." He smiled at Clara and then walked out of the kitchen.

Ed's talk with Mattie to let Clara accompany him was very hard-pressed. Mattie kept insisting that someone would probably recognize Clara, and then she would have to go to jail for what she had done. It put a fear in her that she felt deep in the core of her being. She just couldn't let Ed take her. Ed had talked and talked, telling her that he would make sure Clara was not left alone, and if anyone approached her, he would be able to take care of the situation. He kept assuring Mattie everything would be all right. Ed told her that it would be a good experience for her to see what was beyond their home. Finally, Mattie gave in.

"I can go? I can go?" she repeated, hardly believing she had heard right. She spun around the kitchen. She quickly put the pans in the cupboard and went to her room. She took the paper out of her pocket and put it in the hole by her bed. "My secret." She smiled and then left the room.

Clara was becoming bored riding in the wagon. They had gone deeper into the woods during the first few days. At first, seeing other people amused Clara. At some homes, there were children younger than she was. They would stand around the wagon looking at her. Clara just looked back. No one spoke, and after a few minutes, the children would walk away, becoming interested in other activities.

It took so long to get from one home to the next. They managed on some days just to reach only two homes.

"How far do we need to go?" asked Clara.

"It will be a while yet."

"Pa, did you get schooling?"

"Why you askin'?"

"Was wonderin.'"

I Be Emma

"I got schooling until I got to be a little older than you. My pa got sick, and I was the oldest of my brothers, so I had to quit."

"That how you got to learn to read?"

Pa nodded his head.

"Pa, can I learn to read?"

"I reckon."

"Can you teach me to read?"

"Now, you know how Ma feels about that."

"Yeah, but she's not here. Would you try now?"

"What you wantin' to know?"

"Everything."

"When we settle down for the night, we can start then."

"Thanks, Pa." She silently repeated the letters that Marissa had shown her, and before long, they had stopped at another home.

Pa had explained his travel route to Clara. They would be going to the homes that were not close to towns. Once he finished with them, they would be going towns to general stores. He said there would be things that she would see that she could never imagine. And how right he was.

Traveling out of the woods and onto a gravel road, Clara saw her first automobile. She was startled to see it coming at them. She wondered how a big black box with wheels could go down a road without a horse. She had the luck of seeing three of them.

The next amazing surprise was seeing a town. More than one building was standing along the road. There were people all over.

Pa stopped the wagon in front a building and jumped from the wagon. He took an armful of brooms and went inside the building.

Clara jumped from the wagon and followed him. She stood in the doorway, surprised to see a lot of different things in one room. She slowly walked in farther and looked from one showcase to the other. There were small painted boxes, watches, small fancy bottles, lace and ribbons, plus so much more. Clara couldn't look at everything at once.

At one end of the store were brooms, hoes, and rakes. Across from them were dresses and hats.

Look at all the cloth. And the boxes and the cans... and there are dresses over there, she said to herself. With all the things to look at, Clara didn't know where to start. She decided to look at the dresses.

Such pretty colors. So many of them, and there be shoes.

She went over to the rack of shoes and ran her hand over them. Dare she hold one? She slowly took a shoe from the rack and held it. *What would it be like to wear this?* she wondered.

"Clara, you be putting that back and come here."

"Yes, Pa." She slowly put it back. She tried to look at everything she passed as she walked to Pa.

When I get done being hitched to Bennie, I be coming to this town and live here and buy everything I see, she decided. *People who live here be lucky, and I want to be lucky too.*

"Pa, be there other towns like this that we be going to?" Clara asked once they were back in the wagon.

"Yup, we be going to four more towns."

"Really? Will they be like this town?"

"Yup."

"I can't imagine there be others."

"The county has more than one town. The last town we be stopping at is where we get winter supplies to take home. Your ma be right happy about that."

Clara sat contemplating what else she was going to see and hear. "Can I go with you next time again?"

"I reckon you can." Pa reached into his shirt pocket, took out a paper, and handed it to Clara. "See if you can read what's on that paper. This be our supply list. You sure were quick on learning, so I want to see if you can figure it out."

Clara looked at it and started to sound out the letters. She was able to understand two words, but the rest she couldn't read.

"That be right good. You learn good."

Clara wanted to tell him about Marissa, but she held her tongue. She didn't want anything to stop her from seeing her and having her as a friend.

That night when they set up camp, Pa showed her the alphabet, which she had already memorized, and how to read words. She took in as much as she could.

"My, this sure be a big town," Clara exclaimed the next day. "So many buildings and those automobiles. I never see'd so much."

They slowly made their way to the general store. This store was bigger than the other stores that they had stopped at.

Clara tried to sound out the name *Higgins General Store*. She wasn't sure she was saying it right. "I need to write it down."

As Pa was unloading brooms from the wagon, Clara asked him if she could buy some paper. He said that would be all right. He told her it could be her birthday present, since her birthday was only a week away.

Ever since Clara could remember, her presents were the leggings that she wore in winter. She had never received anything else. She was so pleased that she gave Pa a hug.

Clara went in with Pa. She walked through the store and found what she was looking for: the paper. She made note of what she had picked and then walked back to Pa.

"I found the paper I be wanting."

"We get it when we get our supplies. Right now, I be doing business."

Clara took a look at the store manager. He was a big man with a thick mustache, the ends reaching down to his chin. He gave her a smile and then turned back to talk with Pa.

"I be out sitting on the bench." She turned and headed to the door.

After making her way to the bench, she sat and looked around, taking in the sights.

There be so many people. Where they be coming from? she thought.

People looked at Clara as they passed by. A few women shook their heads, disgusted by her appearance, which she didn't seem to notice.

What Clara did notice was a lady standing a few feet away from her, staring at her. She pretended not to see her. She turned her head the other way. After a moment or two, she looked back and saw that the lady was still there. Two children were now standing with her.

Bess hadn't paid much attention to the girl sitting in front of the store until she got a bit closer. Her steps slowed down and finally came to a stop. Her breathing became a little faster. Her mind raced.

Emma, she thought. *Could this be Emma?* She wanted to run to the girl. *She looks to be about the right age that Emma would be. Same color of hair. I need to calm down. I can't scare her and have her run off.*

"Mother, come on," said Daniel, Bess's son, tugging on her arm.

Bess had forgotten about Becky and Daniel for a moment. "You two go on inside," she said. "Here—take this and get yourself a stick of candy. I'll be there in a bit." She reached in her purse and took out a coin for each of them. She kept her eye on Clara, hoping she wouldn't leave.

I Be Emma

Daniel took Becky's hand, and they went inside.

As Clara watched, she realized that the children were younger than she was. She was amused to see short pants on the boy and wondered why his pant legs were only to his knees. He wore leggings just as she did. She watched as the lady took something from her bag that she gave to each of them. Then instead of watching the children go inside, she kept her eyes on the lady. She couldn't understand why the lady just stood there looking at her.

The lady came closer and said, "I'm sorry to stare at you, but you remind me of my little girl. You see, I had a little girl named Emma. Emma had brown hair like yours. You even have the dark brown eyes like Emma. That's why you remind me of her. I just feel like talking about her to you. She would be about your age. How old are you?"

"I be ten. I be eleven next week."

Clara noticed the lady flinch, so she slid away from her a little farther down the bench.

"What's your name?"

"I be Clara."

"Clara is a nice name. Are your parents here?"

"My pa be in the store. He sells brooms to people and to stores in towns." Clara tried as best she could to make it sound like it was an important job. "He makes good brooms."

"I'm sure he does."

To her surprise, the lady sat down.

Bess Taggert was drawn to her the minute she saw her. For years, she had looked into the faces of little girls, hoping to see Emma. This girl sitting beside her seemed to scream Emma. She looked at her again.

Dear Lord, she thought. *Have I found her? She has Emma's eyes.* She also noticed that the girl was poorly dressed with no shoes. Her hair was uncombed and in a long braid. *What kind of life have you lived?* she thought. Somehow she had to look for the Taggert birthmark, which was located behind the left ear. Her husband's family carried this birthmark for years.

"Where do you live?"

"A long way from here," was the reply. "We be traveling for days and days. We be going home tomorrow."

Bess felt she was losing time and tried to figure out a way to find out more about this girl. She noticed the wagon had a broom in it.

"Would you show me the broom that's in the wagon?"

Clara nodded and headed for the wagon. She reached in, took it out, and handed it to Bess.

"Pa must have forgotten that he left this broom in the wagon."

Bess tried to be interested in what she was holding, but it was hard to look away from the girl.

"My, what a sturdy broom. I bet it does a good job."

Clara nodded. "You be wanting to buy it?"

"Why, yes. I think I will."

Clara turned to go inside the store.

"Wait."

Bess hesitated for a moment.

"Come sit beside me, Clara," she said as she walked back to the bench.

Clara did as she was told.

"Emma was my little girl a long time ago. She disappeared, and I can't find her. I have been looking and looking." Bess felt as if she needed to tell Clara everything she could about Emma. She wasn't sure if this was Emma or not, but she had to take a chance. Maybe by telling the girl about Emma, a memory would pop into Clara's mind.

I need to try anything, she thought. She wasn't going to let this opportunity go by just in case this was Emma sitting beside her. Bess trembled inside.

"Emma had a dog named Dodger."

"Dodger?" There was a pause. "Dodger," she said as if pondering that name. "I have no dog. It just be me, Ma, and Pa."

Bess kept going. "Emma and Dodger were good buddies. Dodger was a good dog. Emma would get mad at him sometimes when he dug up the dirt in the potato patch. She would scold him by telling him he was a bad old dog." Bess gave a little laugh. "She really loved that dog."

"Where be Dodger?'

"Old Dodger died two years ago. Emma would be so sad if she knew."

"I be most sorry you missing your little girl. I hope you find her."

After an awkward pause, Bess said, "My, you have such long hair and in such a nice braid. Turn your head and let me take a look at the braid."

Bess held the braid in her hand, and just as she was about to look behind Clara's ear, the door of the store slammed shut.

A man came out of the store carrying a big box. Clara had turned her head to look. "Oh, Pa. This lady be wanting to buy a broom. You left one in the wagon."

Bess looked at the man, who had a slender build. He had dark brown hair with a little gray showing about the ears and a beard that outlined his jaw and chin. Like Clara, he was shoeless.

"Why, yes, sir. I can tell this broom would do a very good job." She stood up and walked to him by the wagon.

"Well, thank you, ma'am."

"Listen, there are neighbors of mine that can't come to town often. Would you be interested in traveling out my way to sell your brooms?"

"Well, that would be right nice. I can always make more brooms. Next year, I be coming around again. Looks like this here broom's been awaitin' for you."

"That would be wonderful if you would come my way." As Bess started rummaging through her purse, she asked, "Do you live far from Jaspar, Mr. . . . ?" She waited for a reply but didn't receive one. She looked at him after finding a piece of paper and pencil and started writing. "Let me write down where I live and my name. I live on Logger's Road about ten miles from town. There's a big red shed sitting to the right of the house. If you can't find my place, just ask anyone along the road for the Taggerts; they'll know who we are. Just go about a mile south out of Jaspar and look for a turn that goes to the left of the road. It's a small curve, and the road then curves again around some trees."

Bess wrote the instructions down and her full name. She gave him the paper and paid for the broom. She tried one more time. "Thank you, very much, uh, what was your name again?"

"I be Ed." He quickly turned and told Clara to get into the wagon. Pa and Clara said their good-byes and left.

Bess watched them ride away. A whole year would have to go by before Bess would see Clara again.

I can't wait that long, she thought. She turned and went inside the store. She approached the owner.

"Sam, do you know the name of the gentleman that sold the brooms to you and where he lives?" she asked.

"Sorry," Sam replied. "I just know him as Ed. I don't know where he lives either. Why?"

"I just need to talk to him again."

I Be Emma

Bess took Daniel aside and told him she needed to do an errand and to wait for her there at the store.

She turned to Sam. "Is your wife here? Would she be able to watch the children for me? I need to go to the sheriff's office."

"Mable's in the back room. She isn't too busy right now and can look after the children for you. And as for Sheriff Taft, he isn't here. He stopped here to tell me that he was going out to old man McGregor's place. McGregor had come into town to get him. Seems that old man McGregor and Carl Bingham got into some type of dispute about a couple of McGregor's horses getting shot. Claims that Carl did the shooting."

"Do you know when he'll be back?" Bess asked. "I would like to see him as soon as possible."

"Doubt you'll see him anytime soon. It's quite a ways out to McGregor's. He probably won't be back until later today. Julia McKay should be there now operating that there phone switchboard. Sheriff Taft's office is in the same place. Maybe Julia would know something."

"Thanks, Sam."

As Bess walked out the door, she heard Sam call for Mable. She took another look at the road that Ed and Clara rode out of town on and saw a tiny speck in the distance.

I need to get to them before they disappear, she thought.

She ran to the sheriff's office and found Julia sitting at the switchboard.

"Julia, can you tell me when Sheriff Taft will be back?"

"He didn't say. I rather doubt he'll be back soon."

"Do the McGregors or the Binghams have a telephone?"

"Let me check the listings," replied Julia. "Hmm... I don't see a listing for either of them. Is there something I can help you with?"

Charlotte Pritchard

"No. I know he has a car and was wondering if he would be able to drive me out of town a ways. I need to get in contact with someone. It'll just have to wait, I guess."

Bess left and walked back to the store. Before she went inside, she looked down the road and saw nothing. Disappointment set in again like it had so many times before when she thought she had found Emma. *A whole year*, she thought. *That's too long to wait.*

With deep sadness, she slowly opened the door to the store and walked in.

"Here, you take this paper that lady gave me and put it in your pocket. I got that paper you wanted. It be in the smaller box."

Clara took the paper from Pa and put it in her pocket. Then she crawled over the seat to retrieve the tablet of paper that was her birthday gift from Pa.

When she sat back down on the seat, Pa handed her a pencil. "You need one of these to write with."

"Oh, Pa, this be the best present I could get."

Pa had whittled away the wood around the lead so Clara was able to use it right away.

"What be the name of that store?"

"Higgins. You think you can write it?"

"Hmm . . . no."

Pa spelled it for her as she carefully wrote it down. She looked at it and memorized it. For some reason, she wanted to put down that she had talked to a lady there.

"How do you write, 'talked to lady'?"

"Now, why would that be interesting?"

"This lady talked to me about her little girl that she be looking for. I be sad that she can't find her."

Pa started to spell out what Clara had requested but got as far as 'talked to' and then stopped. He became quiet. He told

I Be Emma

Clara that he needed to think and figure out his sales and not to ask any questions.

"But, Pa—"

"Quiet, girl, and let me think."

Clara became quiet as well. She thought about what that lady had told her. She had never heard such a sad story. She sounded out the word "lady" in her mind and wrote what she thought it was.

She was going to write about her adventures someday. Maybe she would be a book writer when she lived in the big town.

Upon their return, Clara managed to hide the tablet and pencil from Ma. Ma was happy to see her and Pa. She said it had been lonesome without someone around the house, although Ida had spent the days and nights with her, helping with housework. The women followed this arrangement whenever Ed made his trips, because one of Mattie's greatest fears was being left alone. In return, Mattie and Clara would stay with Ida for a few days and help her with mending or with canning meats and vegetables.

In fact, Mattie was so happy to see them she gave Clara a quick hug. It surprised Clara enough to give her a hug as well. The moment seemed a little awkward, and they became quiet.

"I . . . I need to get back to the kitchen," Ma stammered. "Ida be canning all the tomatoes we have." She walked into the kitchen.

Clara looked at Pa, and he gave her a wink. Mattie was one not to show emotions very easily. She did love Ed and Clara, but her demeanor was that of a strong person.

Clara wasn't able to meet Marissa after returning from traveling with Pa. The days were getting colder and shorter,

Charlotte Pritchard

making it near impossible to get away from the house. When Clara had free time from chores, she practiced everything that Marissa and Pa had shown her. It wasn't easy getting Pa alone to ask him if the words she had written were actually words. She would sound them out and write them down but wasn't sure if they were correct. She kept at it until she had a whole page of words. She also kept the note from the lady. For some reason, the meeting with her was haunting Clara. Some of her dreams were of trying to find Emma. Shouts of Emma's name echoed in Clara's head. She tried to forget about them, but it was becoming harder. She dreaded going to sleep, knowing that another dream awaited her.

Before the winter snows set in, Ed, Frank, and Bennie went on their annual deer hunt. Frank and Bennie would butcher and dress the deer and then hang it in the smokehouse. By Christmas, the meat would be ready for the two families to share a meal together for the holidays.

"Pa bought this material from town," Ma told Clara. "You growing so tall, you need a new dress."

Clara looked at the pretty red cloth with tiny flowers on it. "I really be getting a new dress?" she said as she ran her fingers across the cloth.

"You sure are. You just be getting taller and taller. I even found some lace that Aunt Polly gave me. I was thinking that I be putting some around the collar."

"Oh," Clara said, taking the lace from Ma. "It be so beautiful." She held the lace to the cloth. There was a loud knocking at the door. Ma went to the door, and there stood Frank and Bennie Stoddard and another man that Mattie didn't recognize.

"Well, it be time you get home. Where's Ed?"

I Be Emma

Frank and Bennie just stood in the doorway. Neither would look at Mattie.

"Well, speak up. Come in, and don't let all that cold air come in with you." Ma stood aside. The strange man came in first, followed by Frank and Bennie.

"My name is Ben Drake. I'm the county sheriff," he said.

Mattie's heart dropped to her feet. A sheriff at her house meant that he had come for Clara. But why now? How did he know about Clara unless someone had told him about her? *Ed or Ida told him,* she thought. *Why?* Her mind raced. She wasn't going to let anyone take Clara from her—not after all this time. She had to think of something to make the sheriff think he was mistaken about Clara.

The sheriff asked, "Do you know Ed Collins?"

"Well, yes . . . he be my husband, and why would you be at my house? What's this about?"

Frank spoke up. "Mattie . . ." He hesitated. "Ed be dead."

"What you jawing about? Where is he?"

"He be dead, Mattie. We was hunting that deer, and we all saw it at the same time . . . and we all stood up at the same time . . . and we all shoot our guns . . . and well . . . Ed had stood up in front of me, and when I shot my gun, Ed fell." Frank couldn't look at Mattie and hung his head.

"I'm investigating the incident and needed to verify that you're his wife," said Ben. "Your husband is at the mortician's in Mount Olive. I'll need you to sign these papers for the mortician."

She wasn't able to respond to what Ben had said. She couldn't move and felt as if she had been nailed to the floor. She just stared at Frank. She started moaning. The moaning grew into a scream.

"No!" she shouted. "You be lying. My Ed not be dead."

"Mattie, I be so sorry."

"Where he be? I want to see him." Mattie rushed to the door. Ben and Frank quickly stepped in front of her.

"He be with the undertaker now. I didn't want you to see him until the undertaker make him look nice and laid out for you," Frank said as Mattie tried to push him away from the door.

"Ma'am, you can see him tomorrow," Ben said. He turned to Frank and said, "When you bring her into Mount Olive tomorrow, just have her sign the papers at the mortician's. She isn't thinking straight now."

Frank nodded at the sheriff as Mattie moved away from him.

She made her way to a chair and sat down. She had a look of disbelief on her face. Frank walked toward her. "Ida be coming in a bit. She says she'll take care of things for you." He was at a loss for more words, and after an awkward hesitation, he turned and went out the door with the other men following him.

Clara was shocked. "Pa be dead? Pa be dead?" she repeated to herself. She looked at Ma. Ma hadn't moved. She went to her and knelt down beside the chair. She couldn't think of anything to say. She put her hand on Ma's knee. Ma slowly looked down at her hand and then at Clara. She started crying. The crying got harder and harder. After a few minutes had passed, Ma stood up.

"Your pa be dead." Clara stood up as well. Ma looked at Clara, and in a hard, angry tone, she repeated, "Your pa be dead." She gave Clara a stern look and then took her by the shoulders and started shaking her. "Your pa be dead," she said in a louder voice, still shaking her. Suddenly, the shaking stopped, and Clara felt a sharp slap across her face. She looked at Ma in disbelief. Never had she been slapped before.

I Be Emma

"Ma be going mad," she whispered.

Clara stood there rubbing her cheek as her mother started crying again. She left Ma standing there. There was knocking at the door. Ida stood in the doorway, and Clara was relieved to see her. She had no idea how she was going to handle Ma, especially after what just happened.

Ida came in, and when she saw Mattie, she went to her and threw her arms around her.

"There, there, Mattie. I be here now, and I be taking care of things for you."

Ida's large frame engulfed Mattie as they held on to each other. Her scarf became undone and fell to the floor, exposing her gray hair braided into a coil around her head. Her weather-worn face didn't hide the grief she felt as she comforted Mattie.

Clara watched the women holding on to each other, swaying back and forth. She left the two of them and went to her room. She closed the door and then let the grief take over.

Ida stayed with Mattie and Clara for the first week after the funeral. As time went on, Clara could tell that Ma was slowly resenting Ida being at the house. A slow anger was building inside Ma. Clara didn't know the cause of the anger until she was awakened in the wee hours of the morning a few days after Ida had gone home.

"Clara, wake up." Ma stood over Clara's bed shaking her arm. "Clara. You get up now. We need to be going."

"We be going where?" Clara couldn't imagine where they would be going at such an hour.

"Never you mind. Just get those clothes on and get Jezebel hitched to the wagon. Go, before the sun gets up."

Ma pulled Clara out of bed and pushed her toward the chair where Clara's clothes lay. Ma started digging through the drawers and stuffed whatever was in them into a sack. Clara quickly put on her clothes.

"What you be doing?" Clara asked in confusion.

"Never mind. Just get going."

Clara went out into the cold night air. She noticed the wagon was up by the house. She couldn't see into the back of the wagon but knew that Ma must have been busy putting things into it.

What Ma be doing? she thought as she got Jezebel and hitched her to the wagon. She started walking back to the house just as Ma was coming out. She pushed the sack at Clara and told her to get into the wagon.

Ma went back into the house and then quickly came out with two blankets.

Clara couldn't image why they were going away and why Ma was in such a hurry.

"Ma, where we be going?" Clara asked.

"We be getting away from here. Going to my kinfolk up north. I lived with my Aunt Polly and Uncle Mack after my folks died and before I got hitched to your pa. We can stay with them and take care of them since they both be old."

Ma took the blankets and put one across Clara's lap and then covered herself. "Not going to stay here near that Frank Stoddard. He done kill my Ed. I can't be forgetting that. They be my sworn enemy now."

With that being said, Ma took the stick and gave Jezebel a poke to get her to start moving.

They moved along slowly. Ma kept talking, and Clara listened.

"We be going north along this here trail that takes us to a gravel road up yonder. That road is too open, and I don't want to be seen. I can't let any of them Stoddards know where we be headed. Once we get on that road, we travel a bit, and just where the road meets the river, we take a dirt road that follows the river. We be more in the woods then, and no one can see us."

"How long do we stay at Aunt Polly's?"

"We stay there for good. We never go back. I won't live near my enemy."

Never go back? Clara thought. The thought of not seeing Marissa saddened her. She sat in silence.

"There be two barrels on this side of the road. That be where we go to get off this road." Ma pointed to her left and told Clara to watch for them. "Once we get on that road, we can stop a bit, but not too long. Can't let those Stoddards catch up with us."

"Why do you think they be coming after us? You be like a scared rabbit."

"Me and Ida had words. I told her what I thought of her and Frank and Bennie. I said that Frank ought to be hanged for killing my Ed. She tried to tell me that it be an accident, that Frank wouldn't have killed Ed for anything. I told her that be a lie, and she got angry, and I got angry, and it just got worse. Told her that you weren't going to get hitched with Bennie and that you were too good for someone as dumb as that boy. I told her that he was only good enough for someone just as dumb as him. I just be afraid they come and take you away with them. They were very happy that we made an agreement for you and Bennie. Well, that's not going to happen."

Mattie had another reason for leaving. After she and Ida had argued, Ida told her that she would notify the sheriff and let him know that Clara had been kidnapped. If Bennie and Clara did marry, then Ida would keep quiet. But Mattie had to keep her promise. This put Mattie in a panic. No one was going to take Clara from her. Over the next few days, Mattie came up with the idea of living with her aunt and uncle. She never explained her past to Ida, so she had no idea where Mattie had come from. Ida only knew that Mattie's parents had died and that Mattie had been taken care of by a relative. Mattie felt satisfied with her idea and knew that Frank and Ida would have no way of knowing where to search for her. They would leave in the middle of the night preventing someone from stopping them if they left during the daylight hours.

The sun was starting to come up and cast long shadows of the trees across their path. It felt as if they had been traveling for hours before the gravel road appeared before them. Ma steadily maneuvered Jezebel down the hill and then onto the gravel road that led them north. Once they got onto the road and in the open, Mattie became nervous. She looked around her as if expecting Frank Stoddard to come out of nowhere and stop them. She poked Jezebel a couple of times, trying to get the mule to move faster. Instead, it felt as if Jezebel were barely moving. She knew it would be some time before she would make it to the dirt road leading to her aunt's house. She told Clara to get the rifle behind the seat. Once she had it, she put it across her lap, feeling confident enough to ward off anyone, even a Stoddard, who would dare try to stop them. She was a good shot and had hunted with her father many times. She could outshoot any of her brothers and even her pa.

 They finally made it to the dirt road. Ma again maneuvered Jezebel onto the dirt road instead of taking the turn on the gravel road. Again they were heading north along the dirt road. The day was winding down, and the sun was beginning its descent. Ma figured they had better make camp once they got out of sight of the gravel road. She felt safe now that she and Clara were in the shelter of the trees.

I Be Emma

They made the campfire, ate, and then bedded down for the night. Clara had unhitched Jezebel and tied her to a tree where there was a patch of grass that Jezebel could graze on.

In the morning, they slept a little longer than Ma had intended, but Ma was glad for the extended rest. She figured they had a few hours left of traveling before they came to Aunt Polly's. She didn't feel as restless as yesterday and took her time getting Jezebel hitched to the wagon.

Once this trip was over, she would start making plans for Clara and her. She would try to find a young man, one that would have money, for Clara to marry. She wanted to live more comfortably and not as poorly as she had. Her plan was to live with them and be well taken care of as she became older, and especially not to be left alone.

The thought of being alone terrified her. She remembered being left alone at the age of five, when she and her parents were traveling by train from Virginia to Tennessee. Her parents thought that one or the other had her by the hand when they boarded the train. In the bustle of the crowd to get on the train, she was pushed back. Before the last of the crowd boarded, the train started to move down the track. She started running down the boardwalk, yelling for her mother.

Once inside the train car, her parents were pushed along. They were pushed onto seats and then realized Mattie wasn't with them. By the time they notified the conductor, the train was traveling at full speed. The train wouldn't stop. When they reached the next stop, the ticket office telegraphed the previous station. Mattie was sent on the next train, accompanied by an elderly couple, and was reunited with her parents.

Watching the train moving away from her had sent her into a panic. The elderly couple that accompanied her to the next stop tried their best to comfort her. Nothing helped. She never wanted to feel that way again. She was determined never to be left alone again.

The dirt road followed the river as they continued to head north. The dirt road changed into a gravel road as they neared Aunt Polly's home.

The Pickrell farm, thought Mattie. *Not much farther*. To her surprise, the farm now belonged to a Dr. Neil Gehring, as indicated by the sign on the side of the road. *I guess some things do change. Nothing can always stay the same.* She hoped Aunt Polly had not moved elsewhere. That thought had never crossed her mind. She had no idea where she would go if Aunt Polly wasn't there.

They finally arrived at Aunt Polly's home. It was nestled in a grove of trees and was larger than the house Mattie and Clara had come from. Mattie looked around. Everything seemed the same since she was last there fifteen years ago. To her relief, Aunt Polly was standing near the house as Mattie led the mule to the front of the house. Mattie took a good look at Aunt Polly as she came toward them. She appeared frail, but there was a little bounce in her step as she came closer to Mattie.

"Mattie, I do declare. What a surprise. What brings you here?" Polly took hold of Mattie's arm.

"Oh, Aunt Polly, I know this is sudden, but my Ed be dead. I wasn't knowing where to go. I be much obliged if we could stay with you."

"Why, Mattie, of course. You can stay here as long as you want. I would enjoy the company."

"I be much obliged. Me and Clara won't be a bother. We be doing our share of work around here too. Is Uncle Mack here? I need help getting my things out of the wagon."

"Your Uncle Mack died years ago, Mattie. I had no way of letting you know. You never wrote to me. You never let me know where to send letters to. Now, who is Clara?"

"Why, she be my daughter. I thought I had told you about her. I be so sorry about Uncle Mack. It wasn't right not to let you know where I was."

"No, I don't remember any Clara."

Clara was standing by the wagon, watching Ma and Aunt Polly exchange greetings. She didn't move until Ma motioned for her to come.

"This be Clara. This is your Aunt Polly."

Polly walked closer to Clara and took a long look at her before she spoke.

"Well, Clara. I didn't know Mattie had children."

"There's only Clara, Aunt Polly."

"Well, she doesn't look like a Collins, nor a Dunning. Where did she get such brown eyes? Seems like there have always been blue or hazel eyes in the family. Well, none the matter. Come in and sit before you unload your wagon."

The days and months were going by fast for Clara since she and Ma first came to Aunt Polly's. She enjoyed taking care of Aunt Polly's home and completed any task she was assigned with efficiency.

"Mattie taught you well," Polly told Clara. "You are a big help to me."

"Thank you, Aunt Polly," Clara said with a big smile.

Polly had Mattie take advantage of the warm spring day by tilling the garden for her. She stood watching as Mattie finished tilling when she felt a sharp pain travel across her chest. She let out a cry.

Mattie turned to see Polly lying on the ground, clutching at her chest. She ran to Polly and helped to her feet. Clara was at the water pump when Mattie called for her. They both helped Polly to the house and put her to bed.

"My heart," Polly gasped.

"Don't say anything," Mattie told her. She and Clara made her as comfortable as they could.

"Get doctor." Polly gasped again. "Lives down the road. Get him."

"Clara, take Jezebel and get going."

"But which way do I go?"

"Go that way," Polly pointed and coughed. "Only house there."

Clara rode Jezebel to the doctor's house as fast as Jezebel could go. She crossed her fingers, hoping the doctor would be there. She saw a man near the house trimming some shrubs.

She yelled out, and he turned around to see who was coming.

Clara jumped off Jezebel and ran toward him.

"Aunt Polly needs help. She says her heart hurts. You need to come quickly."

"How was she when you left?" Dr. Gehring asked.

"She be hurting bad."

He ran to his wagon. The horses were already hitched to it, and he proceeded to ride to Polly's home. Clara followed him but was soon left behind. By the time she rode up to Polly's home and ran inside, the doctor was with Polly.

She walked up to Ma, and they both sat waiting for the doctor to come out of Polly's room.

The doctor stepped out of Polly's room shaking his head. He stood by the door for a second or two and then turned to Mattie.

"I'm sorry, but I didn't introduce myself. I'm Dr. Gehring. Polly is your mother?" he asked hesitantly.

"No, I be her niece, Mattie. This be my daughter, Clara. We be staying with Aunt Polly now."

He turned to Clara and said, "I didn't mean to ignore you when you came to fetch me. I just felt I needed to get here as soon as possible. Well, your aunt has had a bad heart attack. She may pull through the night and maybe a little longer, but this attack really was a bad one. Make her comfortable, and I'll check back in the morning if I don't hear from you before then."

Aunt Polly did recover, but she became very weak and bedridden. Mattie was her caretaker morning, noon, and night.

Clara took care of the household duties, and at night she would collapse into bed. To make matters worse, her nightmares of finding Emma were coming back. She would toss and turn and then wake to a pounding in her ears. She tried to fall asleep again, but she didn't go into a hard sleep, which she needed desperately. She was wishing she had never met that lady or listened to her story. But every time the dream came to her, she would become desperate to find Emma. There were times she thought she could actually hear someone calling for Emma.

Maybe I be going crazy. It be bad enough to have dreams, but to hear someone calling Emma all day, I just have to be going crazy, Clara thought wearily.

Mattie was having worries of her own. She had no idea what would happen to her and Clara if Aunt Polly died. Where would they go? What would they do? She felt so lucky to have a decent place to live that she would do anything to keep her situation permanent. She knew that her cousin Darrel, Aunt Polly's son, would probably evict them from the house. She tried to talk to Aunt Polly about Darrel, but Aunt Polly was too weak to talk. She hadn't seen him since she and Clara arrived. She had no idea where he lived or what he had been doing since she last saw him.

Darrel was not one of Mattie's favorite cousins, and she was sure she wasn't his. Although he was two years older than she, he had always made her feel as if she were a nobody. She always had the feeling of not being a part of the family and that she was a burden to his parents. He would probably point that out to her if his mother died while in her care.

Whatever information Mattie could get from her aunt was too little to satisfy her curiosity. She decided to go through her aunt's papers to find out if there was any information concerning the ownership of the house if Aunt Polly died. She was so busy tending to Polly's needs that by the end of the day, she was just too tired to do a search.

She decided to try and talk to Aunt Polly again.

Mattie opened Aunt Polly's bedroom door and found her sitting at the edge of the bed.

"Mattie, I want to get up and go outside. Help me get dressed."

"You aren't strong enough."

"Phooey. I want to go outside. I haven't felt this good since the attack, so get me outside."

Mattie took a good look at her. Polly didn't look quite as pale, and maybe the fresh air would do her good. She helped Polly get dressed and took her outside. She sat Polly on the porch swing and covered her with a blanket to help take the chill away. It was a brisk day with the sun shining, but she didn't want Polly to end up with pneumonia.

Mattie sat beside her.

"I'm so glad you and Clara are with me. I don't think I would be here if you wouldn't have been here during my attack. I would like to live a little longer and enjoy as much of life as I can. Granted I don't have an exciting life, but just being able to see another day gives me joy."

"I enjoy being with you too. Clara needs to know what living nicely is like. I hope to have her hitched to a nice young man that can provide a decent place for her." Mattie paused. "Let me ask you about Darrel. You don't speak of him since I came. Where he be? I saw his picture in your bedroom. Did he marry?"

Polly was silent. Mattie glanced at her and noticed she had a pained look on her face.

"You be okay?" Mattie got up and wrapped the blanket more tightly around Polly.

"I'm not cold. He was killed in the war. My only child is gone. It's hard to talk of him even still. I keep looking for him to come home. I think that's what killed your Uncle Mack. He grieved most dreadfully. He never got over it. It's a horrible thing for your child to die before you." She put her hand to her face for a moment. She then looked at Mattie and gave her a weak smile. She patted Mattie's hand. "Yes, I'm so glad you're here."

Mattie was silent. She had not known about Darrel. With a feeling of relief, she was glad she didn't have to face him if Aunt Polly died.

"I think we ought to go in. It feels like rain," Polly said as she got up.

Mattie let out a big sigh of relief. *Me and Clara won't have much to worry about now*, she thought as she followed Polly into the house.

"Girl, you be as slow as molasses getting this wash hung up," Mattie said irritably. She and Clara had spent most of the morning washing clothes, and this was the final wash that needed to be hung out to dry.

Clara hadn't slept well during the night. She was trying to find Emma again. It just repeated itself over and over. *Can't that girl be found?* she angrily thought. She was so tired that she thought she was hearing someone calling for Emma as she was hanging up the wash. She was so deep in thought that she didn't realize that she spoke aloud.

"Find who?" asked Ma.

"What?"

"You said, 'Find her.' Who? You dreaming?"

"I don't know." Clara felt she needed to tell someone about her dreams. Maybe if she talked about it, it wouldn't haunt her as much.

"Ma, I be having a dream that keeps repeating itself over and over. When I was traveling with Pa, there was a lady that sat and talked to me. She told me that she had a little girl named Emma and that she be looking for her for a long time. She said I reminded her of Emma."

As Clara kept talking, Mattie froze. *Oh, no. This can't be happening.* Mattie's mind took her back to the events of that day when she first saw Clara.

Ida was taking her daughter, Sarah, to the train station in Jaspar. Sarah was leaving for school in Chattanooga. Ida wanted company, so she asked Mattie to come with her. Before the long ride home, they stopped to have a lemonade. They were discussing a shorter way home when a gentleman who had overheard their conversation interrupted them. He had suggested another route that would shorten their traveling time by half a day. Mattie remembered some of the route, and she remembered the road as Logger's Road. It was along there that Mattie saw the little girl. She was sitting on the steps of a porch.

She and Ed had been trying to have children, but she never carried the babies to full term. She had come to the conclusion that they would never have children, but when she saw the little girl, her maternal instinct set into motion.

It isn't fair that we don't have a child, she thought as she looked longingly at the little girl. *I want that girl*, she thought half-jokingly. A second later and with more conviction, she thought, *Yes, I want that little girl.*

Without any idea as to what would happen next, she told Ida to stop the wagon.

"Ida, will you stop the wagon now?" she said more strongly.

She jumped from the wagon before Ida came to a complete stop. She noticed a dog with the girl and grabbed a portion of their lunch to get the attention of the dog away from the girl. Mattie was surprised that the dog didn't bark. She motioned for the girl to come to her. The girl just sat there looking at her. Again, she motioned for her to come. Once the dog came toward her, the girl followed.

It felt as if time was moving very slowly as the girl and the dog walked up to her. Fear set in. The mother could come out of the house any second and catch her trying to take the child.

"Mattie, what are you doing?" asked a stunned Ida. "Get back in the wagon."

Mattie ignored her. "Do you want to play a game?" she asked. The girl nodded her head. "Well, come with me, and I'll tell you how to play it." The girl said nothing. Mattie quickly picked her up and put her in the wagon. She took what lunch she held and let the dog sniff it. She then threw it into the field, and just as she figured, the dog went for it.

"Get going," Mattie ordered.

"What are you doing?" Ida asked again. "You take her back to the house now. The mother could come out at any moment. What are you thinking?"

"No. Get going and hurry up about it." Mattie looked back at the house and saw no movement or any signs of activity.

"Get going now," she ordered more sternly.

Once the wagon started moving, Mattie smiled at the little girl and started to explain the game to her.

"Your mother wanted me to play a game with you. We be going on a wagon trip. We be going to my house to play. It be a while until we get there. So don't you worry; everything will be just fine."

Mattie knew she played her part well. She promised most anything to Ida, even the marrying of Bennie and Clara to make her go along with her scheme. Satisfied that Ida was pleased with this plot, they kept going.

Mattie told Ida to take a different route to avoid the main road. She knew in her heart that someone would soon be looking for the child.

Putting that to the back of her mind, she thought of how to explain to Ed why she did what she did.

"Mattie, take her back. You be not in your right mind." Ed was still in disbelief from all that Mattie had told him. He stood there looking from Mattie to the child. At least the child had stopped whimpering since he came in. "This be not right. This be not right," he emphasized again.

Mattie stood there looking at him with the determined and stubborn look that Ed knew too well. Her arms were crossed in front of her as if daring him to make her change her mind.

In a more demanding voice, he told her to take the child back.

"No," Mattie replied. "I be your wife now for five years, and I cannot give you a child. Well, we have one now, and there's not a thing you be doing about it. She's our daughter."

"This be not right, and you know it, Mattie. You be taking her back. You cannot be thinking that she be our daughter. She has kinfolk that she belongs to, and they be looking for her right now. I cannot let you do this. I just cannot." Ed gave a stern look at Mattie, but she held her ground.

"Ida should have stopped you. Does Frank know? What will people think?"

"What people? We don't live near anyone for them to be wondering. As for Ida, we done make a deal. When Clara turns fifteen, she be Bennie's wife. You know Bennie be not quite right. There be no gal wanting him. Bennie be real good to Clara. He would build her a nice house, and we all can live together. Then we be taken care of in our old age. Besides, Frank probably be knowing about now. Ida was to tell him that my cousin from Jaspar told me to take care of the baby because she be a widow now and can't be taking care of all her children, especially this here young one."

"You have no cousin there," Ed replied.

"How would anyone be knowing that?" Mattie snapped back at Ed. "There be nobody around these parts to care what we do."

Mattie and Ed's voices were beginning to get louder, and this started the little girl to whimpering again.

"You be upsetting the child, Ed. This talking be over with now."

He squatted down beside the chair she was sitting in. "There, there, little darlin'," He whispered to her. "It be all right."

The girl was softly whimpering and just looked at Ed. Ed was going to pick her up, but she started to move away from him. He stopped and again whispered to her that everything was going to be all right.

"Her name be Clara. Since you be her pa now, you better be calling her by her name. She be your daughter now."

Mattie picked up a pail and said to Ed, "She be wanting to sleep now. You take her and rock her while I go and get some water from the well."

There was a tenderness on Ed's face as he approached the girl. Ed slowly put his arms around Clara, picked her up, and headed for the rocking chair. She didn't struggle, and by the time they sat down, she was resting against Ed's chest and falling asleep.

Mattie headed for the door. She turned around and looked at Ed and Clara.

This be easy now, she thought. With a smile of satisfaction, she walked out the door.

The memory faded when she heard her name.

"Mattie?"

She turned to see a man standing near the gate. She couldn't see who it was because his hat sat low on his head.

"Mattie?" he asked again. He opened the gate and took off his hat. "Do you remember me?"

"Jimmy? Jimmy Wheeler?"

"Yes, it's me. It's been a long time, Mattie. I heard you were here taking care of your aunt, and I had to come by to see if it was true. And here you are."

"Jimmy Wheeler," she said with surprise. "Yes, it sure be a long time." She started to feel as giddy as she did when she first met him at a county fair. He had a wild side to him and a carefree attitude that appealed to her. She had tried many times to get his attention, but he kept her at arm's length. After all this time and distance between them, he still had a profound effect on her. He still had his good looks. She just stood there grinning.

I Be Emma

He grinned back, and for a second or two there was an awkward pause. He noticed the young girl and asked, "Now, who is this?"

"She be my daughter, Clara."

"Well, hello." He approached her, extending his hand. As he shook her hand, he let his other hand slowly rub up to her elbow.

Clara quickly withdrew her hand. He stood there grinning as Clara turned and went into the house.

Jimmy made himself a regular guest at Aunt Polly's. Clara didn't like him since first meeting him. He would watch her and give her a sly grin as if he was planning something. She felt very uncomfortable around him. Whenever Mattie left the room, Jimmy made it a point to get close to Clara with that grin. She would usually manage to get away from him, but when she was unable to, he would start playing with her hair and then gradually let his hand slip down her arm. One time he was able to get his arm around her waist and press her to him.

"What's the matter, girly?" he asked.

Clara started to struggle, and when his hold got tighter, she stomped on his foot.

Once his arm released her, she ran from the room.

After that, she stayed as far away from him as possible and made sure she was never alone with him.

"Clara, please, I just don't have the strength to be listening to you now. Aunt Polly be feeling poorly, and she has a temperature. I'm going to need you to fetch Dr. Gehring."

"But, Ma—" Clara answered with determination.

"Don't 'but Ma' me now."

"Ma, I just be needing—" Clara was cut off by Mattie's sharp reply.

"Why do you have to be so difficult? I don't have time for you now. Get going."

"Ma—"

Mattie's anger peaked. She was feeling the stress of taking care of her aunt and Jimmy insisting they marry and move to Georgia where he was offered a job with the railroad. He was constantly pressuring her to make a decision.

"You know I care about you, Mattie," he would say. "We need to make a life for ourselves. You can leave your aunt in Clara's care."

"I can't leave Clara here and me run off without her. She be my only child. I just can't leave her, Jimmy."

"Well, I can't be waiting too long for an answer. We'll take Clara with us then, if you insist."

"How can you say that, knowing Aunt Polly is so sickly? Don't pressure me, please, Jimmy."

This was something Mattie had dreamed about when she first met him. If Jimmy would have shown any interest in her back then, she wouldn't have married Ed. Now he wanted her for his wife, but she was beginning to think Jimmy wasn't exactly the dependable person that he professed to be. He had said he worked many jobs, but none of them met his expectations. He seemed more of a drifter than someone who could settle down. She was starting to have doubts about him.

Having this pressure on her and with Clara needing something she didn't have time for, she snapped.

"Get out!" she shouted. "The way you been acting lately, I should take you back to your family and let them deal with you!" She was shocked by what she had just said.

"What you be meaning? What family?"

"Nothing. Just go," Mattie replied in a calmer voice. She quickly left the room to attend to Polly.

I Be Emma

Clara watched her walk away. *What family?* she asked herself. She tried to understand what her mother had just said to her.

Her walk to Dr. Gehring's home was taking longer than it should. Clara's mind was trying to figure out what had just happened. *I have another family? Who are they? Where are they? Why wasn't I told about them?* So many questions popped into her head. She felt like she was getting a headache. Ma didn't deny what she said, so there must be another family.

Deep in thought, she finally reached the doctor's home. They left in his wagon, and she was mostly silent on the trip back to Aunt Polly's. She only answered questions he asked about Polly.

When they arrived, Clara went to her room. She started remembering comments made by Aunt Polly and the lady that was looking for Emma.

I don't have the same eyes as the Collins or the Dunnings. I have the same eyes that Emma has, and I remind the lady of her. I remind the lady of her. She repeated that again and again. She lay down on the bed and started crying. *Who do I be?*

She felt exhausted and fell asleep. The dream of Emma came to her again. She found herself crying this time instead of shouting out for Emma. "Nobody will find me," she kept saying. She was now calling out for her mother.

"Clara, Clara!" Mattie was shaking her arm, trying to wake her. "You be having a nightmare. Come, get up and help me with supper."

Mattie started for the door but stopped quickly when Clara asked, "Who do I be?"

Mattie slowly turned with a smile on her face. "Why, you be Clara. You be Clara."

"No, Ma. Who do I be?" Clara asked again.

"You be Clara," Mattie answered more sternly. "You be Clara."

Charlotte Pritchard

Clara's mind reacted to Mattie's answer. She had heard that from Ma before. A quick memory flashed before her eyes. She was being held down sitting on a chair, crying, and hearing "You be Clara" over and over.

"Enough of this," Mattie said. "We be starting supper now. You peel those potatoes," she said to Clara as she went into the kitchen.

Clara went about preparing the supper in silence and was silent through supper as well. She finally excused herself, telling Mattie that she wasn't feeling well.

She sat thinking about the vision she had of sitting in a chair. She tried to remember more but was so exhausted she fell into a troubled sleep.

"Where are you, Emma?" a woman's voice was calling.

"Here I am."

"Emma."

"Here I am." She started crying and was running. She just kept running in a wide circle. "Nobody will find me. Here I am."

"Emma, where are you?"

"Here I am," she kept calling out, running in a circle. Suddenly, a big, yellow dog started running with her. She felt happy, but she kept running in a circle.

"Don't let Dodger get mud all over you. He was digging in the potato patch again."

"Okay, Mama." She still was running in a circle, and just as suddenly as the dog appeared, he was gone, and she was crying again, calling out, "Here I am."

Her dream now took her to being held down while sitting in a chair. Someone was saying, "You be Clara," over and over.

"My name is Emma," she cried.

"You be Clara."

"Emma," she whimpered. She tried to get up from the chair, but she was tied to it.

50

I Be Emma

She woke up, startled. *I remember now. Ma had me tied down and was yelling at me to be called Clara. I be Emma. I be Emma.* She got up and started pacing back and forth. *I be Emma. That lady was my mother.* She tried to remember her face. It seemed so long ago, and she wasn't able to see her clearly.

She lay back down and tried to imagine what it would be like to have the lady as her mother. She finally fell into a comfortable sleep.

Clara was finally beginning to remember things as the days went by, and her attitude changed with Mattie. *How dare she take a child from a mother?* She wanted to get away from her. She wanted no part of Mattie. She was beginning to hate the fact that she had called her Ma. She realized too that she probably would have attended school. To know that she had been forbidden by someone who was not her mother was very upsetting to her.

She became anxious to see the lady again. At night, she lay awake thinking of a way to get to her. She didn't want to wait any longer.

I want to see her. I need to get to that store where I first saw her. I don't know how else to find her.

The tablet that Pa had given to her was left behind when she and Mattie left the house so long ago. She had the name of the store written down and where it was located. She knew her first stop was to go back to the house before she began her search for her mother.

The idea of escaping Mattie obsessed her thoughts daily. She figured that now would be the time to run away, with Polly being sick. Mattie was too busy with her to pay any attention to Clara. She gathered items that she would take with her and put them in the shed until she was ready for them. She had sewn one side of an opening of a flour sack to another opening of a flour sack. She would use this as a saddlebag to throw over the horse that she planned on taking from Dr. Gehring. She didn't want to ride Jezebel because she was too slow. She knew it was wrong to take the horse, but the faster she could get away from Mattie, the better.

Finally the night came for Clara to make her escape. She knew that Jimmy wouldn't be coming because Aunt Polly took a turn for the worse, and Mattie was by her bedside most of the day. The doctor had come and told Mattie that Polly's time was near. When the doctor left and the house became quiet, Clara waited. She checked Aunt Polly's room and found that she and Mattie were both asleep. The only sound was the raspy breathing of Aunt Polly.

She quietly made her way to the back door and outside. She ran to the shed and gathered her belongings.

The walk to the doctor's house took longer than she wanted. By the light of the full moon, she was able to find the horse in the barn and slowly made her way to him. She didn't want to alarm him and have him make noise as she climbed over the gate to his stall. She grabbed the reins that were hanging on a post by the gate. She tried to ease her nerves by talking to him in a soothing voice. She was amazed that he allowed her to throw her bundle of possessions over his shoulders. She guided him to the gate, and they made their way out of the barn. Once she was on the road, she mounted him. Her journey had now begun.

Her sense of direction guided them to the river that she would follow to get to the main road. She would stop there and rest, but right now her nerves were taking over, and guided by the full moon, she was able to keep the horse in motion. The more distance between her and Mattie, the better.

The sun was rising when she finally came to the main road. Everything looked familiar from when she passed by there over a year ago. The two barrels were still in place. She

I Be Emma

went back into the trees a ways. She walked to the river to let the horse get his fill of water. Once he was satisfied, she walked back to a small clearing and tied the horse to a sturdy branch before she wrapped herself up in a blanket and slept sitting up. Her sleep was interrupted by falling over from her sitting position. She decided she better keep moving, although every bone in her body was telling her to lie down and sleep.

On the main road, she wasn't under the cover of the trees. She felt so exposed and was afraid someone would stop her since she was traveling alone. She had the horse gallop as much as possible to get across the road quicker. After traveling much of the morning, she finally spotted the wagon-tracked road that led to the house.

Once on the wagon road and surrounded by trees, she stopped to let the horse rest. She took the blanket and wiped the lather that had built up on the horse. She knew it sounded silly, but she apologized to him for making him run so much. It wouldn't be too much longer until they reached the house.

It was early evening by the time she reached the house. Not much had changed since she and Mattie left. The chickens were gone, but everything else seemed the same. The bushes had grown over part of the porch. The screen door was gone, but the inner wooden door was still there.

She went inside to her room. She was glad she was here despite all that happened. She was so overcome with fatigue, she allowed herself to drift to sleep. She knew she had time now to get her papers and start another journey to find her mother.

She awoke refreshed and hungry. She went into the kitchen and unpacked the food she had brought with her. She was so hungry but allowed herself to eat just a little so she would have some when she traveled again. She sat and thought about Marissa. She wanted to see her again and felt that she would be able to help somehow.

She decided to stay at the house another day. She wanted to rest as much as she could before she looked for Marissa.

She knew that Mattie would probably send someone to look for her because Mattie wouldn't be able to leave her aunt being so sickly. For now, Clara felt safe.

She found the tablet and all of the writing that she had done just where she had left it. They left in such a hurry that night so long ago she didn't think to take it with her. She practiced the alphabet and pronounced the words she had written. She now had the name of the store and where it was located. This was something she would question Marissa about. At least she could point her in the right direction.

As the day wore on, she fell into her old habits and started cleaning up as much as she could. She got the floor swept, and the wind blew through the open windows, helping to eliminate the musty smell. The air was crisp, and she started a fire in the fireplace. Soon the fire was crackling and gave some warmth to the house.

Clara had just finished her meal when she turned from the table and saw someone standing in the doorway.

"Jimmy," she said in surprise. This was the last person she expected to see. "How did you get here?"

Jimmy stood there with that sly grin of his that made Clara uncomfortable.

"Well, well. Here you are, and your ma is right worried." She started to move toward the door as he was making his way to the table. He stopped but continued talking.

"She was nearly frantic with worry when she told me you had disappeared. She couldn't leave Aunt Polly and asked me to hunt for you. She had an idea that you would be coming

I Be Emma

here. I had a hard time finding that wagon road. I was nearly going to give up finding this place but saw the smoke from the chimney. I figured I had to be close to your old place. If I hadn't seen the smoke, I would be rightly lost. I'm not good at directions. I really didn't want to get lost without seeing you. You're looking good for traveling so far. Thought maybe I would find you all tuckered out and scared, wanting your ma. But you seem to be doing all right. Maybe we should just stay here a few days and play house before going back."

Again he gave her that grin that she despised. She told Jimmy to sit down and she would get him something to eat. He did as he was told. Hunger had overtaken his concentration. As he was starting to sit down, Clara ran for the door. She got outside, but Jimmy grabbed her.

"Let me go," she cried as she struggled to get out of his grip.

"Come on, girl. It won't be so bad."

Just then, a figure came around the house and stopped when he noticed Clara struggling.

When Clara saw Bennie, she called out to him.

Bennie came running and hit Jimmy alongside his head. Jimmy stumbled and released his grip on Clara.

Clara didn't stop to see what was happening. She started running toward the dirt road where she had first met Marissa. When she reached the dirt road, she stopped to catch her breath. She looked toward the hill and then to the curve of the road that went around the grove of trees. She figured that would have to be the way to Marissa's house, since she always walked in that direction when coming over the hill. She stood there catching her breath when she heard Bennie behind her.

No, she thought. She saw the gun Bennie was carrying. "Where's Jimmy? Did you kill him?"

"No. I just knocked him out good. He be seeing stars and hearing tweetie birds now." Bennie smiled. "Where have you been? You be gone for over a year now. I saw the smoke and figured you and your ma be at the house. Where be your ma?"

"Ma be with her Aunt Polly. She be sick. Ma be taking care of her."

Clara started to back away from Bennie.

"You come with me. Ma be right glad to see you." Bennie grabbed for Clara but missed.

He set his gun down, and Clara started running in the direction of the curve. Bennie cursed and ran after her.

Just as Clara was running round the curve, she noticed two people standing on the porch of a house. She felt a rush of relief and yelled, "Help!"

They turned and looked at her when she called out. The lady pointed and then went into the house. Clara saw her return with a shotgun in her hand and give it to the man. He stepped off the porch and raised the gun into the air. Next she heard a shot, and then the gun was turned and aimed at her.

Hearing the gunshot, Clara stumbled to a halt. She started to tremble from head to toe and began crying. She felt Bennie grab her from behind and pull her close to him.

"Let her go," came a stern warning from the man with the gun. He went closer and again told Bennie to let her go.

Bennie held Clara close to him and whispered, "Don't you worry. I know where you be. Me and Pa will come for you." He let go of her.

Clara turned and watched as Bennie backed away from her, and then he turned and ran off.

Clara felt her legs go weak, and she fell into darkness.

For three days, Clara lay recovering from fever. She woke to find Marissa looking at her.

"Marissa."

"Shh. You lie still. You've been sick. I heard a gunshot and went to see what was going on and saw you fall on the road. I didn't realize it was you until Father had carried you into the house." Marissa tried to fluff the pillow and tucked the blanket around Clara. "I thought I would never see you again. I looked for you and even went on the path that you take to get to your house. I found it, and there was no one there. Where have you been? You've been gone for so long."

"Ma and me went to stay with Aunt Polly. Aunt Polly be sick, and Ma be taking care of her. Ma was going to stay with her forever, and I would never see you again. Oh, Marissa, so much has changed."

"Well, you can tell me later, but right now you rest. Just one thing though, when you were with fever, you kept saying something about a paper. You need to get a paper."

"Yes, I left it behind. I had no time to get it, and I need it to find my mother."

"Your mother? You just said your mother was with your Aunt Polly."

"Help me, Marissa."

"You just lie back. You're too tired."

Clara lay back on the bed and watched Marissa leave the room. She fell asleep knowing she would be safe from Bennie and Jimmy.

Over the next week, Marissa and her parents, George and Jennie, heard the story that Clara had to tell. Clara found out that while she was recovering, there were visitors looking for her. Bennie and his father had come to take her back to their home but were turned away with the story of her being in the care of a clinic in another town. George and Jennie Campbell knew they would come again.

George offered to take Clara to find her mother. They found it unforgivable for a child to be taken from her mother.

When Clara felt better, she made the trip back to the cabin. Marissa and her father accompanied her. Clara gathered her possessions. She took the tablet and showed Mr. Campbell the paper that had the store's name and where it was located.

"That's about a two- or three-day ride from here. We can make that trip easily. It won't be long now," he said with a smile. He handed the tablet back to her, but it dropped before she was able to grasp it. As she picked it up, a paper fell from it.

"Wait—this fell out." Marissa bent down, picked up the paper, and handed it to Clara.

Clara looked at it.

"Oh, Marissa, this be my mother. When Pa and I traveled with the brooms, this lady wrote down where she lived so that Pa could sell brooms to her. I need to go to her."

"Let me see," George said and took the paper from Clara's shaking hand. "You're very lucky. This will help find her quicker. I say we get things together and start heading for your home."

Mrs. Campbell took a dress of Marissa's and altered it to fit Clara. They also gave Clara a pair of shoes and socks. Marissa suggested they cut Clara's hair.

By evening, a new Clara approached the dinner table with her new look.

"Why, Miss Clara, I do think you are the prettiest girl here tonight," Mr. Campbell said.

Clara blushed and smiled brightly. She felt like a new person.

"We're all going to go with you to meet your mother. We'll make it a holiday."

Clara couldn't help but blush a deeper red. She smiled again and sat down at the table.

"We're going to stay at my brother's on the way to see your mother," added Jennie. "It will probably take another day to get to Jaspar. We'll stop at the store that your father and you had stopped at when you first saw your mother. Hopefully the store clerk can give us clearer instructions to your home."

"My home," whispered Clara. "Can this really be happening?"

"You're a very lucky young lady," said Jennie. "It will certainly be a happy occasion for you."

The journey was now coming to an end. They turned onto Logger's Road. It was just as the store clerk had described to George. The road did take a slight turn and curved behind some trees. Everyone stayed alert to make sure they saw the curve and didn't keep driving along the main road.

Clara's stomach was nervously fluttering. She was going home. Ten years had passed, and she was finally going home. Doubts were beginning to take over.

"Would they have forgotten me by now? What if they decided they don't want me?" asked Clara. She was feeling uneasy.

"I can't imagine a mother and father forgetting or not wanting their child." Jennie tried to reassure her and put her arm around Clara. "It'll be okay." She gave her a quick squeeze and smiled. "Don't worry."

Clara was worrying and couldn't stop trembling. She felt as if she could scream.

As she was trying to calm herself, she could see a barn coming into view from behind the trees. The store clerk had said to look for a red barn, and there it was. The house soon appeared after that. Now she was just a few moments from seeing her parents.

They pulled into the yard, and they all climbed down from the wagon. George and Jennie approached the house, with Marissa and Clara behind them, staying a ways back.

Clara started trembling more. She started crying softly. She looked about her to see if anything was familiar to her. Nothing stood out to make her feel as if she had been here before. It was as if she were looking at the place for the first time.

George knocked and then knocked again before the door finally opened. A boy of about ten years of age came out first, followed by the woman whom Clara had seen at the store two years ago.

Clara watched as they talked and then saw her mother look her way. Her trembling worsened, and her crying was becoming a moan. She heard her name being spoken.

Clara watched her mother coming toward her. She tried to take a step toward her but was unable to move.

"I . . . I . . . be . . . Emma," she stuttered through her crying.

Clara felt arms go around her. Clara kept hearing her name over and over as she was being hugged. She noticed a man come out of the house.

This must be my pa, she thought. She watched him coming toward her and then buried her face into her mother's shoulder, crying harder.

Jake had come out of the house. He saw Bess hugging a young girl. He turned to George with a questioning look.

George simply said, "Your Emma is home."

"What? What did you say?"

"Your Emma is finally home."

Jake slowly walked up to Bess and Clara. He couldn't take his eyes off of the girl.

"Bess, what's happening here?"

I Be Emma

"Jake, our baby's home," cried Bess. "She's finally here with us. Oh, Jake. Look at her. She's such a beautiful young lady. She's here, Jake. She's finally home."

Bess stepped back from Clara so Jake could see her.

Jake stepped closer. "She's so much older than our Emma."

"Take a good look at her, Jake. She's Emma. This is our Emma. Of course she's older. Emma would be older by now. She was only three years old when she was taken."

Jake stepped closer. He took hold of Clara's arms to stop her from shaking.

Clara couldn't stop crying and tried to look at Jake.

Jake raised her chin up and looked harder at her. To Clara's surprise, he turned her head and touched her left ear. It felt as if her ear was being folded.

"Oh my, oh my," Jake said. "Bess . . . Bess, our Emma's home. She has the Taggert birthmark."

Bess nodded. "After all these years, my prayer has been answered. I don't have a heavy heart anymore. Let's go into the house, and you can meet your sister and brothers."

Once more, Clara felt arms go around her. How long they stood there and hugged her, she had no idea.

She felt a great relief knowing that she was finally home. No more worries. She was home.

Clara met her sister, Becky, and her brothers, Daniel and Jacob.

"We knew we had another sister," Daniel stated. "I didn't think I would ever see you."

"Why is your name Clara?" Becky asked. "Where did you live?"

George cleared his throat. Everyone's attention turned to him.

"I would like to tell you about what happened. I think Clara will be able to fill in on what I left out. But I'll start and let her catch her breath."

When he finished and after Clara calmed down, she took over. She told them how she found out that she was Emma. She mentioned to Bess that they had met once at the Higgins store in Jaspar.

"I knew it. I just knew it. I had this strong feeling it was you. I wanted to follow you. The only thing that threw me off was when you said your birthday was in the week after I met you. Emma's birthday, your birthday, is in May, not October. I had asked the store clerk the name of your father, but he just knew him by the first name. He had no idea where you lived, only somewhere in the backwoods. He didn't even know what direction you had come from.

"After you left the store, I went to the sheriff's office to have him follow and stop you before you had gotten too far from town, since he had a car and I didn't. But he wasn't in his office. He was out of town settling a dispute between two neighbors. He contacted me later that day, but the chance of finding you by then was scarce. He said he would do a search early in the morning and perhaps come across your campsite. He didn't find you. It felt as if my heart was torn from me again. You were so near.

"I would go to the store often to see if you and your pa had been there, but you never came. I started to believe I imagined the whole thing. But I never gave up. Honestly, from the day you were taken and after all these years, I just knew I would see you again. I just didn't know when. Your father and I have missed you so much.

"Well now," Bess stated. "I must say I like your hair short." She gave a little tug to Clara's hair. "You had such a long braid back then. You're a really beautiful young lady." Bess gave her a

I Be Emma

quick hug and then turned to George and Jennie. "I'm sorry, but I don't remember your names, and I haven't been introduced to this young lady." Bess made her way to Marissa.

"I'm George Campbell, that's my wife, Jennie, and our daughter, Marissa. We live north of Jaspar, up by Mount Olive, about twenty miles from here. Marissa met Clara about two years ago and mentioned her to us, but we never met the parents. We know a family, the Stoddards, that live around us but didn't realize there was another family living close to them. I didn't know that Clara's pa was a broom peddler. He never came to our door." He hesitated. "I'm kind of wondering if you're going to press charges against the mother. She should be held accountable for what she's done."

"I don't want to see her again," Clara adamantly stated. "She can stay where she be. I hope she feels right poorly knowing she'll never see me again."

"I can understand you feeling that way, but something should be done, don't you think?" asked Jake.

"She can be miserable for the rest of her days and die of a broken heart. That would be something that could be done." Clara paused and then said, "No, I don't want to see her. Leave her be in her misery."

There was silence.

"I . . . suppose," Bess answered slowly, "we could do that and leave it alone. What do you think?" She looked at Jake.

"We have her back now . . ." Jake shook his head. "We're going to need to find her, and Emma will have to identify her, since we have no idea what she looks like. Do you know about where she's living now?"

"Please, just let it be," Clara begged. "I don't want to ever see her again. Let's just be a family now. Don't let me see her, please."

"This is really upsetting you, isn't it?" Bess asked.

"Can't she just be left alone? I be wanting to forget her and never think about her again. Please let her be." Clara gave a small whimper as Bess put her arms around her.
"Jake, let's forget about this. To tell you the truth, I don't really care to see her myself. Let's just be a family like you said, Emma. Does anyone have objections?" Bess gave a little laugh as she looked at everyone. She then took her hand, lifted Emma's chin up, and said, "We love you, Emma."

Clara settled into her home and never imagined she could feel such happiness. She felt safe and really loved by the people she had been taken from, even though much time had passed.

Clara told Bess about her desire to go to school. Bess decided to first teach Clara as much as she could at home. Clara learned quickly, and after three years of learning at home, Clara entered high school. She went on to college in Chattanooga and became a teacher.

Clara never lost contact with Marissa. Marissa was a nurse in Chattanooga when Clara entered college. They shared an apartment and only parted when Clara married.

In time, Clara all but forgot the people she had met after she was taken. She had no desire to ever see Mattie or to contact her. She was looking toward the future and wanted to experience as much as she could after being denied living the fulfilling life that she now knew.

The day after Clara left Mattie, Aunt Polly died. The fear of being left alone started to overwhelm Mattie. She kept vigil for weeks, sitting on the porch and looking down the road, expecting to see Jimmy and Clara coming home. They never came. The neighbors started calling her Mad Mattie. They didn't interfere with her when she started wandering the woods, calling for someone who would never come. Mattie's voice still echoes across the hillside calling, "Clara!"